THE PARTING GIFT

Noel Coughlan

THE PARTING GIFT
Copyright © 2015 Noel Coughlan

This is a work of fiction. Names, characters, places, and incidents either are the product of the author's imagination or are used fictitiously, and any resemblance to actual persons, living or dead, events, or locales is entirely coincidental.

Cover by Paula Becattini
Edited by Finish The Story
      http://www.finish-the-story.com/Editing.htm
Proofreading by Proofed to Perfection
      http://www.proofedtoperfection.com/
Formatting by Polgarus Studio
      http://www.polgarusstudio.com/

Published by Photocosmological Press http://photocosm.org/

Paperback Edition: 978-1-910206-08-9

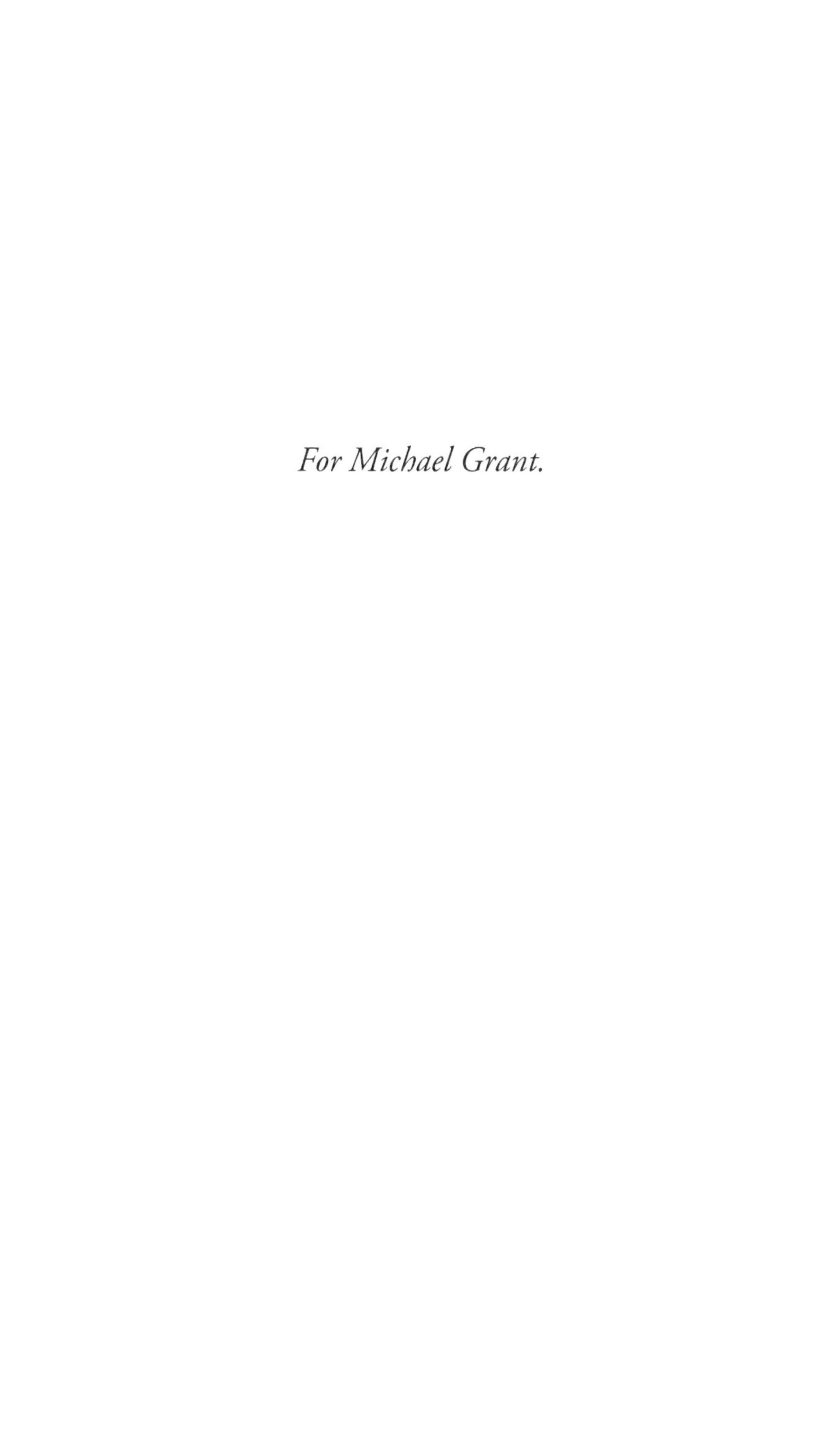

For Michael Grant.

I

Certamen stared at the wooden floor as his mistress, the Sable warrior DarkGlad, scourged the Purpure, but the hands pressed to his ears could not block out the roars the creature retched forth as the whip stripped its flesh. The monster had brought this on itself. This was not the first time that, in the depths of night, it had started shrieking for no reason and roused either DarkGlad or her husband.

Certamen shuddered at every stroke. No matter how he might be favored, he was not immune to the whip if he upset his owners.

The Purpure's desperate screeches dulled to groans and then simpers, but the whipping continued. Was DarkGlad going to beat the creature to death? An involuntary scream gurgled in Certamen's throat. Suddenly, the lashes ceased.

"Certamen," DarkGlad said, panting.

Head still bowed, his eyes strained upward to glimpse the Sable's face. The symptoms of her exertion were obvious—the sweat drenching her round, vermilion face and the dark blotches on her cheeks. A scowl hooded her black eyes.

She handed Certamen the whip. The greasy warmth of the Purpure's blood smeared his pale yellow fingers as he gathered the cords.

DarkGlad parted her mess of black hair, revealing the black geometric pattern on her forehead that represented the face of her race's creator, the Dark Light, Solanum.

"Clean it before you retire for what little is left of the night," she said as she flexed her hand. She turned to the Purpure. "And as for you," she growled as she kicked it in the ribs, "if you ever again disturb the Dark Light's time with your screeching, I really will give you something to cry about."

The other slaves hid in the gloom beyond the candle. Most pretended to sleep as if it were possible to be so oblivious to the creature's tortured cries. Certamen's heart contracted as a baby's sudden cry drew desperate shushes from its mother.

DarkGlad answered his anxious glance with a sneer. "An infant's wails won't carry to my hall. Unlike this brute's howls." The Purpure shuddered as her boot struck its side yet again.

After she departed, the slave house exhaled a collective breath. The other slaves stretched their limbs and shimmied about their straw mattresses. They were all Mixies—Argents or Azures stripped of their patrons' colors. Their clumsy features provided no clue as to which race each individual belonged. Even their skin colors, a meaningless spectrum of browns and pinkish whites, could not be relied upon to differentiate them. Perhaps they themselves no longer knew. They certainly did not care.

Certamen was the only Or on the farm. His flaxen skin and extra thumb on each hand set him apart.

Labored breaths drew his attention to the Purpure. The creature no longer inspired dread as it had during the Light War. Its limbs were manacled to the floor, so it was only free to turn from side to side. It could not even wipe away the frothy drool smeared across its face. Its gray, hairy back was raw, crisscrossed with welts. Its deadly horn was long gone, sheared off by its captors. Its large, shining eyes drizzled tears. It was so pathetic it was hard to believe it belonged to the same species that had massacred most of Certamen's race.

Having cleaned the whip, Certamen stepped outside the slave house. The bloody sickle of the Red Light, Gules, hung in the sky, tingeing the night an eerie scarlet. As always, its presence was a taunting reminder of past suffering, like a scar that would not properly heal. Its barren deserts had been where the rival divine Lights fought for supremacy. There, the Ors had failed their god. Defeated and enslaved, they had lost everything, even their purpose.

The journey from Gules to Elysion had been like waking from one dream and falling into another. Fragments of memories remained—the glass tower extending like a lithe arm out of the desert into the ruddy sky, the steaming waters of the Rainbow Sea, the desolate mountains beyond it, the first marvelous green shoots peeping up through the scorched earth, and then the first glimpse of Elysion, a lush salad of forests and grasslands. Yet most of the journey was an elusive phantasm that flickered in the periphery of Certamen's consciousness.

He didn't bother to secure the door and lock the slaves inside. The Sables' equine brethren, the jet-black Cavals, were a greater deterrent to escape than any bolt. The herd grazing nearby consisted of four mares, a foal, and a stallion with a broken horn. The adults watched Certamen as he passed them. He answered their intimidating stares with a deferent smile.

Even if a slave escaped the farm, where could he go? The world of Elysion belonged to the Sables. It was their prize for winning the Light War. Though Elysion was the embodiment of the Green Light, and though other Lights contributed to its beauty, the Dark Light was its undisputed ruler. His presence saturated Elysion. Scratch the surface, and he was waiting, lurking in every crack and crevice. From dusk to dawn, the world was wrapped in his shadow. He was inescapable.

The Purple Light tinted the horizon. Instead of retiring to his resting place in the Sables' hall, Certamen loitered outside to witness the dawn ripen. Gradually, other Lights revealed themselves. The soft luminescence of the Blue Light diffused across the firmament; the Green Light stirred in the drowsing countryside. The White Light, lord of storms, had spared the new day from his sourer manifestations, but he, too, was present as languid veils of mist reclining here and there in the meadows.

These haughty deities were beautiful and powerful, and Certamen murmured thanks to them for choosing to bless this morning, but they were not the reason he declined his bed. The blushing sky to the east promised a visitation by the Golden Light, Aurelian. Certamen prayed to his creator not with his mouth but his heart. It chirped with the birds petitioning the sun to rise. The first tongue of golden fire pierced the sky. Aurelian—god, light, and sun combined—started his slow ascent into the heavens.

Certamen's soul opened like a flower; every sense stretched and tilted to catch his god's radiance. Here was his dearest treasure, the certain proof of his creator's resurrection. Of course, Aurelian was also in bondage. The Golden Light's defeat in the Light War had made him a slave of the Dark Light.

In a sense, it was comforting that Aurelian accepted his vassal status. The world had an order, albeit one not to everyone's liking, and order ensured peace. An occasional whipping weighed little against the slaughter meted to the Ors on Gules.

Certamen was happy with his lot. The Sables treated his race particularly well. The Ors' continued fidelity to their Light had earned their masters' respect. The delicacy of the Ors' features, the luminosity of their hair and skin, also charmed the Sables. The Ors' near annihilation by the Purpures in the Light War meant only the highest-ranking Sables owned them. They had become possessions to flaunt and covet, like living precious stones.

On some farms they were pampered like children, allowed to play away their days. On others, Ors lorded over their fellow slaves and allotted rewards and punishments according to their whims. The privileges granted to Certamen by his owners were modest in comparison, but they were sufficient to raise him above his fellow slaves. That was enough for him.

The other slaves, bleary-eyed and yawning, gradually filed from their quarters and set about their chores. The Mixies pretended to ignore Certamen as they trundled by him, their contempt glinting in their eyes.

Prodded by three wary Mixies, the Purpure shuffled outside. Shackles and chains deprived the creature's movement of its native, murderous elegance. It greeted the day with a surly growl. Its guards examined the lacerations on its hide and declared it fit to work. It was led away to the fields to pull a plow for the day.

II

Certamen was about to start his own duties when he spotted a chariot drawn by two Cavals coming toward the farm. It was too far away to identify its passenger or the Or running behind it, but Certamen couldn't wait. His masters must be informed immediately.

As he raced into the Sables' hall, he almost careered into PiousNight, DarkGlad's husband.

"Where have you been?" PiousNight growled. "Dawdling about the farm instead of being ready to attend your mistress!" He snatched the whip from Certamen's hands and raised it over his head.

"A chariot is coming!" Certamen pleaded. He raised a trembling hand over his face. The act was certain to further provoke PiousNight, but Certamen could not help it.

The whip wavered. Certamen bowed his head.

"It must be DiligentServant," DarkGlad said.

Certamen glanced up. The whip was cradled in the

arms of its bearer.

PiousNight turned toward his wife. "And it must be of grave import for him to travel during the Dark Light's time."

The chariot halted outside.

DiligentServant leapt down from the car. "Galea, unharness the Cavals and see to their needs."

As he strode over to DarkGlad and embraced her, PiousNight's face twisted.

"How have you been, DarkGlad?" DiligentServant asked. He glanced at PiousNight. "How have you both been?"

"I'm expecting," DarkGlad said, her lips curving into a smile.

PiousNight grinned.

"Congratulations to you both," DiligentServant said warmly. He shook hands with DarkGlad and then PiousNight.

Certamen woke from his daze. It wasn't a slave's place to stand there as if somehow part of the conversation. He stoked the fire and plumped the cushions, then prepared some refreshments for the Sables, all the while glancing at them and listening.

"And the farm?" DiligentServant asked.

DarkGlad shrugged. "With the slaves, it is easy."

DiligentServant's voice quieted. "You're not nervous out here in this wilderness all by yourselves?" he asked.

"We're not alone," PiousNight said. "We have the Cavals."

"You came by yourself," DarkGlad observed.

"I can drive that vehicle as well as any charioteer," DiligentServant said. He flicked a nervous glance at PiousNight. "In peacetime, obviously. I wouldn't have your husband's skills."

PiousNight nodded. A tight smile stretched across his face.

They sat down on cushions, while Certamen poured wine for each.

DiligentServant took a sip, then frowned. "I have something to discuss with you in private."

"Certamen, you can leave us for now," DarkGlad said.

Certamen bowed and left. The dismissal was peculiar. The Sables had always ignored his presence in the past.

He found DiligentServant's Or, Galea, waiting outside. It was strange to see another member of his race after so long. The flaxen face beneath the golden curls hadn't aged in the slightest. Galea's orange eyes sparkled. Looking about nervously, he opened one hand, displaying its symmetrical dual thumbs. With some reticence, Certamen reciprocated. If they were caught making the sign of their god, their owners would give them a severe thrashing.

"It must be three years since we last met," Galea said.

"Have you met any other Ors recently?"

"I met Malleolus, Nitor, and Cor on other farms," Galea said. "I saw Consilium, Auctor, Peritus, and Fulgur when DiligentServant took me to the Champion's palace, but I did not get an opportunity to talk to any of them. I hear the Champion, being ruler of the Sables, retains ten

Ors in his retinue. And you? Have you news of any others?"

Certamen sighed. "Where would I meet them? My masters never bring me anywhere. Not even to the neighboring farms. I am stuck here, surrounded by Mixies, and they make sullen company. They hardly speak to me."

"Your companions are friendlier than mine then," Galea said. "My first day on DiligentServant's farm, my bedding and other possessions were stolen. I searched the slave house but found no trace of them. They were dumped or destroyed. Spite, not greed, was the reason for their theft. I complained to DiligentServant, but he has no interest in the squabbles of slaves. I nearly got a whipping for my troubles."

He shook his head ruefully. "Now I keep what little I have with me, or if I cannot, I hide my belongings in the forest where the Mixies would have to work hard to find them. You know how lazy they are. They often spit at me. I have had to wash their disgusting phlegm from my hair so many times. The dirty beasts laugh about it. They think it is funny. They also hit me when they think they can get away with it."

"I had similar problems here when I first arrived," Certamen said. "Then one night, two Mixies seized me while I slept and gave me a severe beating." With a grimace, he revealed his teeth. "See, they knocked out a tooth. They broke my nose too."

"I noticed your nose was crooked," Galea said.

Certamen blushed. "When DarkGlad and PiousNight

saw me the next morning, bruised and bloody, they were furious. I knew who had beaten me, but for some reason, I shied from identifying them. I claimed I could not see their faces in the dark. DarkGlad whipped Mixies at random until the culprits revealed themselves, and you can imagine the punishment they received for damaging a gift from the Champion. One of them still walks with a limp. Since then, the Mixies here have given me little trouble."

"You were lucky," Galea said. "Well, you were unlucky to be beaten, but the incident was something your owners couldn't ignore. My Mixies are too clever to make that mistake. They do enough to make my life miserable but not enough for DiligentServant to bother to take an interest. I hate Mixies. I can hardly suffer being in the same hut as them, inhaling their stinking breath, listening to their self-aggrandizing lies. They are so sly and deceitful." He shivered. "They sicken me. They maintain such a docile manner around Sables, but behind their backs, Mixies mock their masters with the voraciousness of wolves tearing apart a carcass."

"I don't think Sables are beguiled by their act," Certamen said. "At least, not my masters. DarkGlad often says that Mixies are uninspired workers, easily distracted, prone to slack when unsupervised, and not to be trusted. She says they promise a lot but deliver little."

Galea pursed his lips. "If DiligentServant is aware of their falsehood, he never speaks of it. If he knows, he certainly does not care."

"I've often thought the most damning indictment

against the Mixies comes from their own lips," Certamen said. "Their haste to accuse their own kind of deceit is astounding."

Galea chuckled grimly. "But what would you expect from two races so quick to disavow their Lights? The Sables never asked them to renounce their gods. Yet they discarded their allegiance to their white or blue lord as if it was something they had used to wipe their bottoms."

"Their strange antics at night astonish me," Certamen admitted. "Some whisper gibberish while kneeling, squatting, or standing. Some strike their backs with cords as though their master's whip was not enough. Others occasionally creep into the forest, tie braids of their hair to tree branches, or daub rocks with blood. One Mixy even serenades a star when it is visible in the sky."

Galea nodded. "I, too, have witnessed such odd behavior on DiligentServant's farm. Several Mixies sing to a star as you describe. Others stand motionless with their arms raised above their heads like tree limbs. Such ridiculous nonsense!"

"I would be happy to trade masters if it were possible," Certamen confided. "I am envious of your good fortune to serve DiligentServant. I would be content to bear the cruelty of his Mixies if I could travel like you through Elysion."

"Its beauty makes me sad at times," Galea said. "Had we won the Light War, this land would not be so unkempt."

Certamen nodded. "What news of the world beyond

this farm?"

"Only bad news," Galea replied. "A sickness is spreading through the land. It has killed many Sables."

"Have many Ors died?" Certamen asked.

"No," Galea said, bowing as he kicked the ground. "Ors and Mixies and Purpures appear to be immune. It infects only Sables and Cavals. Our masters are scared. They blame the Purple Light. The victims' skin takes on a purple cast."

He glanced around and said softly, "There is a lot of wild talk." He paused a moment and then whispered, "Some Sables want to kill all the Purpures."

Certamen gasped. Surely such barbarity was consigned to the past, to Gules. The Sables would not sully their hard-won paradise with such a depraved act. "The Purple Light, all the Lights, would punish them," he protested.

Galea shrugged. "The Dark Light gave us to the Sables to treat as they please. If the Sables decide to kill the Purpures or the Mixies or us, no Light will stop them."

"You are certain they intend to do this?" Certamen asked.

Galea opened his hands as he shrugged. "I overheard some Sables discussing it."

"Could be just talk," Certamen suggested, rubbing his chin.

"Could be," Galea admitted. "I am not privy to the mind of the Champion, so how can I be certain?"

Arguing with Galea was pointless. Once his view had fixed, it was impossible to alter.

But Certamen wasn't persuaded.

The Sables must be devising a cure for this sickness. Perhaps they planned some grand sacrifice to appease the Lights. The possibility that knowledge of the disease might embolden the Sables' slaves to rebel was sufficient reason for secrecy. Galea might have overheard some guest at one of his master's feasts—befuddled by drink, no doubt—mutter about killing the Purpures, but the sober majority of Sables would not entertain mass murder as a cure for the Purple Light's plague. How would the Purple Light be appeased by murdering his children?

III

Later that day, as DiligentServant's chariot sped away from the farm, DarkGlad turned to Certamen. "Tell the Purpure's chief handler, Mogrid, I wish to speak to him."

Certamen nodded and turned to go.

"As soon as possible," PiousNight added.

Certamen broke into a trot. The wooden tablet hanging from his neck that identified him as DarkGlad's property slapped against his chest to the rhythm of his stride.

The Purpure's minders were engrossed in playful banter as the creature dragged the plow ahead of them. Over half the field had already been tilled.

Certamen waved as he raced up to them. "DarkGlad and PiousNight want to see you immediately, Mogrid," he panted.

The handlers' merriment ceased. They halted the Purpure. Mogrid, the swarthiest of the three, glanced uneasily at his two frowning companions. He removed his egg-shaped hat and rubbed a hand through his wiry, dark hair. "Keep an eye on the brute and make sure the furrows stay straight."

Mogrid puffed beside Certamen as they hurried back to the Sables.

"You wouldn't know what this is about?" Mogrid struggled out between gasps.

The Mixy's question was as gratifying as it was unusual. If only Certamen had an answer…

"I'm afraid I don't," he admitted.

The Mixy's grunt was followed by a hostile silence.

The Sables waited for them outside the hall. DarkGlad's foot tapped impatiently. "What kept you?" she demanded.

"Sorry, mistress." Mogrid gasped. He bowed as much to catch his breath as to show respect. Strange. The Mixy had never struck Certamen as being so unfit.

DarkGlad crossed her arms. "The Purpure is to be deprived of its food tonight."

Mogrid's eyes narrowed. "Yes, mistress."

"Certamen, I understand one of the children was unwell last night. Seek the mother and learn all you can about its symptoms. Then report back to me."

DarkGlad dismissed the two slaves with a wave of her hand. As the slaves' quarters and the field lay in the same direction, Certamen was forced to be Mogrid's companion a little longer.

"Starve the Purpure," the Mixy murmured. "No reason given. No mention of last night's ruckus, so it can't be for that. The Purpure's been well behaved all day. Not a squeak out of it. I don't like it. Our masters are up to something."

Certamen bit his lip. Mogrid's confidence intoxicated him. Should he mention DiligentServant's visit? "I—"

"I wasn't talking to you, Goldilocks," Mogrid snarled, changing direction in apparent attempt to lose his unwanted associate.

That night, as the whimpering Purpure was chained to the floor, phantom manacles closed around Certamen's wrists.

"Certamen, you will sleep here tonight and keep an eye on the Purpure," DarkGlad said, handing him a whip. "Give it a taste of that if it starts howling." She slammed the door behind her. A bolt made a scraping sound as it slid into place.

IV

Certamen squeezed the whip as his eyes sifted the gloom for somewhere to sleep. He approached a small gap among the prostrate bodies. As he stepped over one lying Mixy and then another, he tensed, ready to lash out at anyone who dared to attack him. He lay down on the hard wooden floor. His neighbors shuffled about. He sat up and raised the whip, but the Mixies were shifting farther away. Being hated sometimes had unexpected benefits. He lay back down and tried to relax.

He shut his eyes, though his grip on the whip never loosened. He flinched at every sound, no matter how innocent. The wooden tablet hanging from his neck pressed down on his chest, adding to his discomfort.

Thankfully, the Purpure did nothing to disturb the Sables' slumber. The creature just lay quietly snoring where it was fettered, too exhausted by its labors to protest its starvation.

A wild scheme teased Certamen. Imagine if he and the

other slaves rose up against their overlords. Or, Mixy, and even Purpure could rule Elysion, and the Sables could serve them, harvest their fields, tend their livestock until the former slaves chose to release their chastened masters. The five races could prosper together as equals, and the Lights would rule them as equals, and Elysion would be a paradise for all the races, not just for the Sables. The peace on Elysion would no longer be enforced by the whip, by fear.

Even the Sables must be afraid. In many places they were a minority, outnumbered by their slaves, and this pestilence spreading through their settlements and farms would exaggerate this disparity further. Yes, the Sables were afraid. Fearful enough to contemplate the Purpures' extermination.

By his inaction, Certamen was complicit in this impending atrocity. He could loosen the Purpure's bonds. The bolt on the door wouldn't prevent it from escaping.

No, it was too dangerous. The creature was likely to react to such generosity with violence. Certamen could not endanger himself and the other slaves. If he had food, he could have snuck the creature a few morsels to relieve its hunger pangs, but food lay beyond the bolted door.

A yell announced the morning. Certamen startled awake. He must have fallen asleep at some point during the night. At least he still had the whip. Drying sweat made the handle tacky.

"Everyone outside!" the cry repeated. It was DarkGlad's voice.

As Certamen queued with the Mixies to leave the cabin, he glanced back at the Purpure. *The Sables are going to kill it. They are going murder it while it is chained to the ground and unable to defend itself.*

Outside, lines of Sables in black armor formed a cordon around the slaves. It was evident from the fearful bewilderment stamped on the Mixies' faces that they, too, realized something sinister was happening. The spears closed around them, hemming them in on all sides. Beyond the Sables, several dozen Cavals watched attentively for trouble.

"Certamen!" PiousNight shouted. He was part of the cordon, unrecognizable in his armor. He reached out a hand.

Certamen smiled with relief. He strode over to his master.

"Give me the whip," PiousNight said.

Surprise and habit made Certamen obey. The gap in the line of Sables where PiousNight had stood closed in an instant.

Three Sables entered the slave house. The Purpure whined pitiably, then fell silent. Chains rattled. The creature stumbled awkwardly through the doorway. Its new handlers, unused to their task, randomly prodded it forward and tugged its choke chain. The Purpure was forced inside the cordon with the rest of the slaves.

DarkGlad stood outside the ring of Sable warriors, elevated above the crowd by her chariot. She waved her arms to demand the slaves' attention.

"You are leaving the farm," she said. "Behave, and no harm will come to you on the journey."

She made a signal with one hand. The Sables' spears drove the slaves forward. The farm and its comforting certainties were soon distant, and Certamen found himself traversing wild countryside as hostile as it was unfamiliar. Slumped in thought, he took little interest in his surroundings. The destination, not the route, was his principle worry. He had feared the Purpure was to be murdered, its race expunged. Now it was apparent the other slaves would share the Purpure's fate.

Escape was impossible. The slaves were unarmed and outnumbered by their guards. Even if Certamen managed to alert the others of the impending massacre, even if they somehow overcame their reflexive aversion to him and heeded his warning, the Mixies were too lethargic to act. They defied their owners with countless small exasperations, but open rebellion was too great a leap for their timid imaginations. Fettered by their docility, Certamen had no choice but to trudge on and pray to the Lights that he was wrong.

A glinting notion relieved a little of his foreboding. If the Sables' intention was simple murder, why did they not dispatch the slaves back at the farm and save themselves all this laborious herding? It was such an obvious question. Why had he not thought of it sooner?

And then, as quickly as hope ignited, it died. If the slaves were killed on the farm, the Sables would have had to remove the corpses from the property. Execution and burial at the same location was more convenient.

DarkGlad's terse speech provided little comfort. She had guaranteed the slaves' safety during the march, but she had mentioned nothing about what awaited them at its end.

The Sables will probably make us dig our own graves.

He seethed at the thought. Could his life have such little value?

Rage pushed him to the front of the column. Warning glances from the lead Sables were all that prevented him from charging ahead. The sooner this journey ended, the better. At least he might be troubled no more by these morbid speculations.

V

Through the morning and hungry afternoon they marched, pausing briefly only once at a rivulet to slake their thirst. As the exhausted slaves arrived at a palisade, evening bled across the sky. Outside, two Purpures whined plaintively as they wriggled against the chains fastening them to posts. DarkGlad's Purpure was prodded over to where a third post was being erected while the rest of the slaves were herded inside to join the multitude of Mixies within. Not one Or stood among them. Certamen was alone.

The pen stank of stale urine. A large trough of sour water sated the newcomers' thirst, but their guards fed them only promises. In the morning, the slaves would have plenty of food. All they had to do was be patient. Some slaves moaned halfheartedly, but most were too weary to protest.

Morning came too fast for tired bodies. The Sables' whips organized the weary slaves into rows.

DiligentServant scrutinized each slave in turn, picking out the lame or otherwise enfeebled. He passed Certamen without a glance. At the end of the inspection, those deemed unfit to walk were taken away.

"Where are you taking them?" Certamen demanded. Fear and impatience got the better of prudence.

DiligentServant strode over to him and eyed him intently. "They will travel in carts. As you are so concerned about their welfare, you can join them."

Two Sables seized Certamen's arms, dragged him from the pen, and forced him into a wheeled cage. The enclosure was already so packed that he had to stand, while the low ceiling forced him to hunch. His companions were heavily pregnant women, recent mothers and their newborns, the crippled, and the sick. The driver ensconced on the roof whipped the two Purpures harnessed to the vehicle, and the cart jolted forward.

A little wriggle room remained in the cage, and the Mixies took turns propping themselves against the lattice of bars to imbibe fresh air through the gaps. Certamen neither asked for, nor was offered, a chance to be part of this informal rotation. He twisted around and breathed through a gap in the ceiling until the awkwardness of his posture became unbearable, forcing him back to stooping. It was impossible to lose himself in his thoughts—the ache creeping up his legs and back, the dew of his companions' breath prickling his skin, the reek of their stale sweat, their bodies jostling and pressing against him.

At noon the cart halted, and the driver fed the

prisoners. Pats of cold gruel were spooned through the bars into their outstretched palms. Determined not to be bullied out of his share, Certamen pushed and shoved and squeezed his hand through the curtain of clinging prisoners to snatch half a handful of precious sustenance. It was sour and hard to swallow, but it satisfied his growling stomach a little. He greedily licked his fingers.

The vehicle moved off again, then halted suddenly. The door groaned open. Mixies disappeared through it, until a path cleared between Certamen and the Sables outside.

"You get out!" one of them roared.

Who was he talking to? Certamen stayed still in hopes that the order was directed at someone else.

Red hands reached inside and seized him. He wriggled against them as they dragged him toward the open door, but he could not break their hold.

"Mind what you're doing!" a male prisoner roared as Certamen kicked in rage.

Hands pressed against his back and shoved him out. A Sable fist eclipsed the sun before it struck his cheek. He spiraled as he fell and landed facedown in the dirt.

A whip cracked, followed by the desperate shuffle of feet. The door rasped and banged as it swung shut.

"That'll teach you to jump when I give orders," a Sable declared.

"You've tasted PureHeart's fist. You'd better get up before you taste his foot," one of the Sable's comrades said.

Certamen stood, his hands brushing at the dirt on his

tunic. "I'm sorry," he said. "Master," he added, a grudging afterthought. His cheek hurt, but he dared not touch it. Showing weakness might invite greater violence. He wistfully watched the cart trundle away.

"Look at me!" PureHeart demanded.

Reluctantly, Certamen obeyed. The Sable's black eyes glared at him.

"Now I have your attention," PureHeart said. "One of your kind has taken shelter in a place we cannot go. You're going to convince him to leave it. He can't escape. If he stays there, he'll starve to death. Don't get any ideas about joining him, either. Even if we cannot reach you, our arrows can. Do you understand?"

Certamen nodded.

PureHeart turned and stomped away. "Take him to the pit."

Hands pushed against Certamen's back, shunting him forward. "Walk straight ahead until I tell you otherwise," one of the Sables ordered.

He obeyed, turning left or right as he was told. The Sables remained stubbornly behind him. He risked a quick glance.

A fist punched his back. "Keep your eyes on where you're walking."

What was the reason for this secrecy?

"Stop!" a voice roared. A sour-faced, female Sable emerged from the thicket. "Where do you think you're going?"

"We brought this Or to talk some sense into the one

hiding in the pit," one of Certamen's guards said.

The female Sable scrunched her nose. "This is a waste of time. We should bury the pit and him with it."

"PureHeart's orders."

The female Sable grunted. She beckoned Certamen with her hand. He hesitated.

"Hurry up!" she snapped.

He approached warily.

Her gauntlet's metal fingers dug into his shoulder. She pointed to the thicket behind her. "It's in there. Follow the cat tracks."

She released her grip. Certamen rubbed his shoulder as he pushed through the dense wall of young trees. Wheel ruts cut a path through the brush. At the end, a huge depression yawned. A fly tickled his cheek. Others hummed around him. He tensed at the stench of putrefaction. He forced a reluctant step forward and then another. What awaited him in the pit?

The buzzing grew louder, the flies more brazen. He shielded his mouth and nose, took a deep breath, and strode onward.

Each step nearer the lip revealed more of the far side of the pit. Certamen shuddered at the realization that the purple flowers peeping from the midst of the black bed were actually hands and faces. Standing on the pit's edge confirmed the bottom was covered with Sable corpses at various stages of decomposition. The depth of the layer of bodies was anyone's guess.

Crouched on an island in this sea of carrion was an Or.

"Hello!" Certamen yelled.

The Or shielded his eyes and looked up. "Who are you?"

"Certamen of the Eleventh Legion."

The Or saluted with an open hand. "Defensor of the Fourth. How did you end up here?"

"The Sables sent me," Certamen said. "They hope I can convince you to leave."

The Or looked about. "Come on down. You see that flat, dark green rock over there? There's a collection of stepping stones over to here."

Certamen descended the crumbling bank and followed Defensor's instructions. The stink was unbearable. It was as if he were swimming through flies as he stepped and hopped from one stone to the next. One rock wobbled beneath his foot, threatening to tip him onto the rotting cadavers, but somehow he kept his balance. Everywhere, dead eyes stared at him.

Finally, he took Defensor's hand and leapt onto his little island.

"They're terrified they'll catch the plague if they come near the pit," Defensor said.

"How did you end up here?" Certamen asked.

"I overheard my masters discussing the removal of the slaves from their farm, so I fled."

"Do you know what they intend to do with us?"

"I'm sorry to say I don't," Defensor said. "I didn't wait to find out. I got all the way here from Bysea, and then I blundered into some Sable hunters. They nearly caught me, but fortunately, I stumbled upon this sanctuary." His opened his arms wide.

"You can't stay here." Certamen spat a fly from his mouth. "This place is a slow death at best."

Defensor grinned. "I couldn't leave, but now you're here… Come closer. They may be watching."

As Certamen leaned nearer, Defensor stuffed something into his hands. Wrapped in rags was something hard—a knife of some sort.

"Be careful," Defensor hissed. "That thing is sharp. It'll slice through you in an instant if you're careless."

"It's a knife?" Certamen asked. Were they being watched? He scanned the pit's rim. If anyone was up there, they were well hidden.

Defensor grinned. "It more than a knife. It's a relic from the Light War. A parting gift from my master."

"Impossible," Certamen said. "It was forbidden to bring such weapons to Elysion."

"My master kept his as a trophy," Defensor said. "He smuggled it to Elysion. I took it from its hiding place. He may not even know I've taken it. Even if he does, he can't openly search for it. The penalty of possessing such a weapon would be stoning or worse. This knife might be our people's last hope, depending on what the Sables have in store for them. You must protect it with your life."

Certamen nodded.

Defensor looked unimpressed. "Promise me in our Bright Lord's name that, no matter what happens to me when we leave here, you'll guard this weapon."

"By Aurelian, I promise," Certamen said. As if his word wasn't enough.

Defensor sprang onto the first stepping stone. "Let's go."

As he bounded to the other side, Certamen tucked the knife beneath his tunic and cautiously followed. The stones were less steady this time, or perhaps it was a trick of his imagination.

Movement in the midst of the cadavers caught his eye. An arm shifted, a plea for help. Someone was alive. The shock nearly toppled him into the mess of bodies. As he steadied himself, he pointed to the arm. "Look!"

A rat peeped out from under it.

"There's a lot of those about," Defensor said. "I'm surprised there aren't more."

Growing nausea hastened Certamen across the stones. Standing beside Defensor, he leaned over and retched. He waited for his empty stomach to stop clenching. Every spasm hurt.

"Lucky those stones were there," he said.

"It wasn't luck. It was me," Defensor said. "I didn't feel safe here. Whatever chance of Sables sneaking down to the edge of the grave to catch me, there's no way they'd attempt to cross to the mound in the center."

They climbed up the slope and followed the cart track through the brush. Through the haphazard screen of branches and saplings, waiting Sables were visible. Defensor winked at Certamen and took a deep breath. They pushed forward.

As Certamen emerged from the thicket, a fist punched his face. He stumbled backward, dazed by the blow.

"That's the wrong one, you fool!" someone yelled.

Their correct target now identified, three Sables surrounded Defensor and punched and kicked him to the ground. Certamen's foot twitched forward. He had to do something, and yet…

The wrapped blade shifted dangerously under his tunic.

"Enough!" the female Sable said.

The other three panted as they stared down at Defensor's inanimate body. He lay facedown.

"Is he dead?" one of them asked.

Another Sable grabbed a fistful of Defensor's locks and yanked his head upward. Defensor roared.

"So, you're alive," the Sable said. "We should've left you down there for the rats. Get up!" He pulled Defensor to his feet.

PureHeart shoved between Defensor's abusers. "Escort them to the pen at Beefield."

The Ors walked in front; the Sables strolled behind. The brush revealed glimpses of black-clad figures pushing piled carts toward the pit.

Defensor tottered dangerously. Certamen wrapped an arm around him to steady him. Whatever awaited them in Beefield, at least he wouldn't face it alone.

VI

It was well into the night when they reached the stockade. After some heated discussion between their escorts and the pen's guards, the doors were opened, and the Ors were shoved inside. His legs aching, Certamen stepped awkwardly through the sleeping Mixies quilting the ground and claimed a small patch of earth into which he and Defensor could curl their frames. The ground was bare, but exhaustion numbed him to its hardness. He placed one arm across his chest to protect the precious knife from thieves.

A prod in his back woke him. His eyes fluttered open. The morning light stung.

"You don't look too happy to see us, Certamen."

He pressed a hand to his tunic. Thank Aurelian, the knife was still there. He looked around to find the speaker. Galea and half a dozen other Ors sat in a circle around him and Defensor.

"This is Taedifer," Galea explained, his finger moving

from one Or to another. "He was with the Ninth. Libamen, Cor, and Malleolus you might remember from the Eleventh. Urbanus and Fidelis of the Third. For those who don't know, this Or is Certamen of the Eleventh. And your friend is?"

"I'm Defensor of the Fourth. And who might you be?"

"Galea of the Eleventh."

"I met your master," Certamen told Galea.

"One thing of which I am sure is that I am nothing to DiligentServant, not even his slave," Galea muttered sourly.

The Ors exchanged their stories. The others' experiences were much like Certamen's. Evicted without explanation from their farms, they had been marching for several days.

"The only thing for certain is we are moving southward," Cor said. "If we keep traveling in the same direction, we'll eventually reach the river Rim that marks the boundary of the Sables' domain. What happens then is anyone's guess."

"*If* we reach it," Libamen muttered.

"We brought a knife with us," Defensor whispered. "A special knife."

Before he could explain further, the pen's gates groaned open, and Sables spilled inside. They picked out the sick and feeble from the crowd and removed them as they had the previous morning. The Sables' whips organized the remainder into orderly lines, each of which was marched out the gates in turn. A row of bubbling cauldrons fringed one side of the road. As the slaves filed past, they received a small loaf of bread as soup was ladled into their bowls.

Certamen sighed. Would he have to hold his soup in one hand?

Someone behind him tapped his shoulder. Winking like a Mixy, Defensor thrust a small wooden bowl at him. "I noticed you had no bowl. This is a spare I found," he whispered.

Back along the line, a female Mixy cursed loudly. She demanded the Sables punish the culprit who had filched her bowl. She even accosted the slaves nearest her, rummaging their persons for her precious vessel. The encircling menace of raised whips quickly quieted her.

As Certamen received his ration, he glanced at Defensor's gleeful face.

"We must look after our own," Defensor said. "Nobody else will."

Certamen buried his dismay with a smile. Mixies hated them. The Ors owed them nothing. They would happily steal from Ors. Why should the theft of this bowl bother him?

They ate as they marched. Distracted by their breakfast, the thread of slaves formed knots, permitting the Ors to travel in a bunch. The soup was watery and the bread stale, but the meal was delicious. Certamen ruefully licked his bowl clean. The food had sharpened his hunger. Cor offered him a chunk of bread. Certamen refused with a hand wave, but Cor just deposited the bread into his bowl.

"Eat it, Certamen," Galea said sternly. "You and Defensor ate little yesterday. You need your strength."

Certamen acquiesced with a nod and started to chomp through Cor's gift. Would anything ever sate this ravenousness?

A chariot sped by them. Somewhere ahead, it skidded to a sudden stop.

"Stop!" The order echoed down the line. The slaves stuttered to a halt. Some sat down to rest, but they quickly rose again as a dozen Sables stormed past.

"Oh no," Defensor murmured.

The Sables formed around their belligerent leader in front of the Ors.

"That's the one," the leader said, pointing a finger at Defensor.

"Are you sure he's your slave, DuskJoy?" one of the Sables asked.

"He's still wearing his tag," DuskJoy grunted, his face burning with barely contained rage.

Defensor groaned. As the Sables closed around him, he made a halfhearted effort to evade them, more of an instinctive recoil than deliberate resistance. They dragged him before his former owner.

DuskJoy flexed the whip in his hands. "Tie him to the tree over there."

"Shouldn't we search him first?" one of the Sables asked.

"No!" DuskJoy snapped. "Tie him to the tree first. I'll search him then."

"I don't know what all this secrecy is about," another Sable muttered.

They bound Defensor to the tree. He stood facing the trunk, his arms stretched around it in a grotesque hug. Defensor yelled as they pulled the rope taut.

DuskJoy waved away the other Sables. He patted Defensor down. He tossed aside a wooden bowl. He whispered something in the Or's ear.

"Did you find what you are looking for?" a Sable asked.

"No," DuskJoy said. He tore open Defensor's tunic with a knife, exposing his back. White scars already crisscrossed the flaxen skin. DuskJoy stepped back and raised the whip.

Certamen flinched at every blow. For two dozen lashes, Defensor kept silent through gritted teeth. The fresh welts on his back quickly merged into a bloody mess. After that, each strike of the whip drew a scream.

The blade beneath Certamen's tunic weighed. If he exposed it, if he revealed the reason DuskJoy had come here, the Sables would turn on Duskjoy. He had committed a crime against the Lights, specifically his own patron deity. The monster would suffer a long, agonizing death.

But DuskJoy wasn't the only monster here. Any Sable could be as violent and cruel. This knife Defensor had entrusted to Certamen might make a difference to the Ors' future. It might ensure they had one. He couldn't throw that advantage away, however much he desired to.

The pace of the blows quickened as Defensor's screams turned to groans. DuskJoy's face contorted into a triumphant grin. Defensor fell silent. His head lolled to one side. His legs were limp. Only the rope pinning him to the tree kept him upright. But DuskJoy gave no sign of relenting. This wasn't punishment. This was murder.

"Enough!" a Sable cried. "Killing him isn't going to get back whatever he's stolen."

DuskJoy panted as he stared at his victim. "Where's the Or who brought him out of the pit?"

A chill passed through Certamen. He glanced around at his friends. How could he slip the knife to one of them unnoticed?

A reassuring hand rested on his shoulder. "I am the one you speak of," Cor said, stepping forward.

"Search him," a Sable said.

"Leave him, ShadowHelm!" DuskJoy commanded. "I'll examine him."

ShadowHelm sneered. "You may be a captain, but you're not our captain. You can't order us about. I want to know what is so precious and secretive that you would go to all this trouble."

"Your captain, DiligentServant, will be informed of this insolence," Duskjoy said. His voice was as hollow as his threat. He watched, trembling, as ShadowHelm and the other Sables searched Cor.

"Found it!" ShadowHelm said.

DuskJoy's eyes popped. He lunged forward. "Give it to me!"

ShadowHelm threw a wooden bowl at his feet. DuskJoy tripped over it. He spread his arms out to regain balance.

"That's not what you're looking for?" ShadowHelm asked, tartly.

The other Sables chuckled.

DiligentServant stomped up to them. "What's the meaning of this delay?"

ShadowHelm lifted his helmet and scratched his black hair. "We were helping the good captain find something he lost."

DiligentServant directed a pointed frown at ShadowHelm. "If we don't get moving, we won't reach the next pen before nightfall. Cut that Or from that tree. You and you"—he pointed to Certamen and Cor—"carry him. DuskJoy, we must have a chat about this incident in private."

While the two captains remonstrated, the slaves were herded onward.

Defensor's head lifted a little, then dropped again. Certamen bent down near his ear. Perhaps Defensor couldn't hear him, but Certamen had to say it.

"I'm sorry," he whispered.

Defensor looked up. "Don't be. You did what needed to be done."

"What did DuskJoy say to you?" Cor asked.

"He wanted to know where his knife was. And… and as he hit me, he said he'd kill me if I didn't tell him where it was. He said… he said in a few days, my death wouldn't matter."

Cor's face mirrored Certamen's shock. What were the Sables planning to do to them?

The knife shifted awkwardly, forcing Certamen to reposition it. Defensor's theft of it had the feel of divine providence, but a single weapon, no matter how wondrous, could not prevail against the might of the Sables.

VII

For three days, the routine was the same. The slaves marched through the day to be incarcerated in a new stockade each night. Bread and soup were doled out in the morning and the evening, bread and water at noon. The companionship of his own kind greatly cheered Certamen, as did Defensor's slow recovery from his whipping.

The Ors were inseparable. They walked together and ate together. At night, they took turns guarding against thieving Mixies while the rest slept in a huddle. As other gangs of slaves merged with theirs, more Ors joined them. For some, the eviction from their farms had been very recent. Others had traveled from the extremities of the Sables' realm—the hem of the Bony Mountains and the coast.

They agreed Certamen should remain the knife's guardian. It was both an honor and a burden. As the days passed, the blade's preciousness grew. This hope wrought of metal was surely a gift of Aurelian, but its promise was tempered by the uncertainty of its purpose. How could a single knife save them?

On the fourth day, just before noon, the slaves entered a large encampment on the crumbling banks of the Rim. They were hemmed in on one side by its sluggish waters and on all others by Sable spears. Above them loomed a large boulder, on which were perched two figures. One was a female Sable clad in armor. The other sat hunched on a black throne, the details of his features lost in dancing shadow.

The Champion.

A peculiar ecstasy gripped Certamen. The knife hidden beneath his tunic could pierce that veil of night. Pressing it against the Champion's throat would be enough to force the Sables' surrender, to wrest freedom for the Ors. This must be why Aurelian had given them this weapon.

There must be some way to reach the Champion. But how could Certamen get past the wall of spears? The cordon enclosing the slaves was six men deep.

Bound Purpures were hustled into the enclosure. Staffs pinned them to the ground as their handlers removed their chains. The Sables withdrew in unison. The Purpures leapt up, their howls brimming with menace.

"The Sables have let the beasts loose amongst us!" someone cried. People began to wail.

As the Ors formed a protective circle, Certamen shook his head at the irony of what was unfolding. His concern for the Purpures' survival had proved to be misplaced. The Sables had intended to use them to massacre the other slaves all along. That was why they had starved the brutes.

He slipped his hand inside the tunic, undid the cloth wrapped around the knife, and gripped the hilt. He had to draw it at the last possible moment. A glimpse would be enough for the Sables to recognize it.

Stones rained down on the Purpures, no doubt to rile them further. No, the battering of missiles was forcing them to retreat. They backed toward the river, turned, and dashed into its turquoise water. They waded across its vast girth, the water reaching their waist and then their shoulders, till the river threatened to swallow them entirely. Some of them emerged on the far bank, only to disappear into the forest. It was difficult to be sure if they had all made it or if the river had swept some of them away.

The woman on the rock addressed the assembly. "I speak for the Champion, paramount servant of the Dark Light, the steward of his people, the speaker of his word, the enforcer of his law, the ruler of Elysion and its peoples. Know this, you children of vanquished Lights—the Champion gives you your freedom. He decrees that the lands on this side of the river Rim belong to the Sables alone. You and your descendants are henceforth banished. The punishment for trespassing is death, irrespective of reason. The ford before you is your means of departure."

The Mixies roared and wailed. Some cried that this was murder. The water was too high. The Purpures had nearly drowned. Others protested their unpreparedness for exile. They had no food or tools, no means to survive in the wilds.

The Champion's voice boomed above them. "Your Lights shall provide!"

Lines of warriors closed like the jaws of a terrible predator, kneading the crowd in on itself, pushing it toward the river.

"Hold hands," Certamen yelled to his companions.

The chain of Ors twisted and strained as panicked Mixies buffeted it. The crowd compressed into a single mass that slid blindly toward the river. Faces were ugly with fear. A man held a screaming infant above his head. Another tried to cling to those around him as he slipped beneath the trample. A woman begged in vain for her missing child.

Water lapped Certamen's ankles. The river washed the crowd apart. Libamen and Cor slowly waded deeper, carefully probing for the shallowest route, stretching the chain of Ors behind them. Certamen fought against the current, his legs struggling to carve labored steps through the icy water. As the water rose, the numbness in his feet spread up his body to his chest. He glanced back at the lines of Sable warriors on the shore sweeping the last of the slaves into the Rim. The river was full of slaves wading, swimming, struggling, drowning.

A Mixy, insane with panic, seized Galea and dragged him under the water. Cor and Defensor, who held his hands, strained to pull him up against the combined force of the Mixy and the river. Breaking the chain, Urbanus rushed to their aid and beat Galea's assailant with his free fist, but the Mixy refused to let his victim go. Twisting one hand free of his neighbor, Certamen drew the knife and pulled the chain after him. The sun flashed on the blade as he thrust it at Galea's attacker. His roar became a gurgle as the river swallowed him. The wounded man drifted away from his victim, a feathery cloud of blood spreading from his corpse.

With agonizing difficulty, the broken links in the chain reformed. The Ors drew nearer to each other. Still clutching the knife in one hand, Certamen held on to the chain with the other. Whatever else happened, he must not lose this weapon.

As they started to move forward again, the riverbed plunged beneath him. The icy waters coiled around him, squeezing his chest, prying at his mouth and nose. He might be still clinging to the chain, but he was too numb to be sure. Lost in the shapeless murk, he thrust the knife upward, uncertain if it reached the surface.

Take the knife. It's more important than me.

The chain refused to let him go. Hands seized him, pulled him upward. His head emerged from the river, permitting him to take a shivery breath.

"Are you okay?" Defensor asked.

Certamen nodded. His jaw shook uncontrollably.

Defensor grinned. "Watch your step in the future."

The water rose until it closed around Certamen's throat like icy fingers. The little wooden tablet bobbed against his chin. The current strengthened. It threatened to lift him off his feet and carry him away, but he put his trust in the hands holding his and pressed on. The water gradually receded, and trembling with exhaustion and cold, the Ors emerged from the river.

A Purpure burst from the foliage.

Certamen waved the dagger at the beast. "You know what this is, don't you? This will cut through you like butter if you come anywhere near us."

The Purpure winced as the sun's reflection on the blade danced over its face. It disappeared back into the forest.

Certamen collapsed onto his knees. His whole body ached.

"Look!" Fidelis cried, pointing at movement in the bushes. Lots of movement.

Certamen stood and readied his knife while the others seized stones and bits of wood.

"Consilium!" Galea cried, pointing to one of the emerging Ors. They were armed with crude clubs.

Consilium, the Legate of the Eleventh Legion, grinned. The disparate clumps of Mixies still struggling across the river, intimidated by the Ors gathering on the bank, veered away to seek another place to exit. So many Ors had not been gathered in one place since they arrived on Elysion.

"Good afternoon, friends," Consilium said. "Welcome to south of the Rim and its freedoms, such as they are."

"Freedom to starve," someone chirped, earning a couple of chuckles.

Consilium's grin didn't waver. "Take heart that it is

little different from the Sables' domain. When the first of us arrived here, we assumed we had been driven into a wasteland, but we quickly realized the boundary of the Sables' domain was as arbitrary as our banishment. The Sables have foolishly given away the world to keep one little corner for themselves."

"Is this your entire number?" Cor asked.

"No," Consilium said. "Others are searching for food or guarding our camp. The Purpures and Mixies infesting this area make it necessary to travel in groups for protection. We come here every day to search for new exiles."

His gaze drifted across the new arrivals. It settled on Certamen a moment before moving on. "Some of you I know—like Certamen and Galea of the Eleventh over there," he said. The acknowledgment was gratifying. "Others are unfamiliar to me."

Consilium greeted each of Certamen's companions as, in turn, they called out their names and their legions.

"Friends," he said sadly. "It is good to honor the memory of your legions. We are all that remains of them. As most of you probably know, I was Legate of the Second and later the Eleventh. Often I weep for our Bright Lord slain on Gules, for comrades and friends swallowed by its hungry sands. But we are more than the vestiges of a dead people. We are a new legion, the last hope for our race. We must depend on each other to survive in this wilderness. The petty jealousies and rivalries that so weakened us on Gules are past."

"Are you the legate of this new legion?" Certamen asked.

"I am," Consilium replied. His voice was cold, even haughty. His misinterpretation of the question as a challenge stung.

"Then I will follow you," Certamen said firmly. Some of his companions echoed his sentiment with more fulsome declarations, others with murmurs. Certamen offered the knife to Consilium. "And this is rightfully yours."

Defensor nodded. "It was a parting gift from my former master."

Galea's murmur was too indistinct to make out the words, but the cynicism in his tone was plain. Certamen's glare warned him to be silent. Regret mingled with pride as Consilium took the knife.

Consilium raised it and studied it. "We must thank Defensor's master if we ever meet him. Thank you, Defensor and Certamen. A fine blade, indeed, this Parting Gift."

Certamen shivered as he and his companions stripped off their wet clothes and donned the spares Consilium's party had brought. It was evident from the faded, dark red spatters on some of them that they had been taken from corpses. It was best not to dwell on the manner by which their wearers had met their end. At least the clothes were dry and warm.

Water spilled from the twisted fabric as they squeezed out their old clothes. Certamen was missing a sandal. He slipped off the other one and drew back his arm to toss it away.

"Wait!" Consilium yelled. "Don't throw anything away. We have so little as it is. We must keep every scrap of civilization we possess."

Certamen's cheeks warmed. Of course, Consilium was right.

As they strolled to the Ors' camp, Galea whispered to Certamen, "Can we trust Consilium? He and the other legates led us to our near extinction."

"Do you want to lead?" Certamen asked.

"Not me."

"Then you, too, must follow."

Galea sighed and said no more.

The camp scarcely deserved the name. The dwellings could have been mistaken for piles of broken branches. Strewn beside a pile of twigs in an unused hearth were a variety of sticks, probably the tools employed in several unsuccessful attempts to start a fire. So this was what freedom was like. It wasn't particularly impressive.

The camp's denizens encircled the newcomers and applauded. Consilium thrust the Parting Gift into the air, and the claps turned to cheers.

"A miracle of the Divine Lights, an edge that never dulls, a blade that never breaks," Consilium said. "With this weapon, this Parting Gift, we can craft a proper bow drill to light the fire. We can make all the tools we need. This instrument of death will be the means of our salvation. It will lift us above the bestial existence of the other freed slaves. It is the means by which we shall build our new civilization."

It was a stirring speech. Certamen cheered with the rest, though his heart was troubled. Despite being fully clothed, a sensation of nakedness pestered him. Only a few days before, the world had been a reassuring order, but now Certamen had been stripped of that certainty. For the first time in his life, he was free.

As the cheers waned, there came a distant cry, a guttural wail, bestial and triumphant, reveling in unexpected liberty.

I hope you enjoyed *The Parting Gift.*

Please check out *A Bright Power Rising* and *The Unconquered Sun*, a duology set in the same world.

It would mean a lot to me if you left an honest review wherever you purchased it, and/or at Goodreads.

If you want to keep up with my future projects, join my email list at http://eepurl.com/OVUjf, follow me on Twitter (@noel_coughlan) or Facebook (Noel Coughlan - Writer), or check out my blog at http://photocosm.org/.

Feel free to email me at noelcoughlan@photocosm.org to ask any questions or comments you have about this book.

Best wishes,
Noel

A Bright Power Rising

Set in the same world as *The Parting Gift.*

AscendantSun's memory stretches back to the bloody birth of the cosmos. Created to serve a dead god, he tired of his empty religion and adopted the faith of his former enemies. Now, a threat from the past is forcing him to choose between his new friends and his own people.

Escaping enslavement made Grael a hero in others' eyes. As everything he has won begins to slip away, he strives to protect his loved ones from both the Elfin invaders and the machinations of his own ruler.

Everyone else considers Garscap's childhood tragedy to be a curse, but he knows it marked him for greatness. Mercenary, manipulative and murderous, he has the mind of a great leader, but not the heart. Will his ruthlessness prove ultimately to be his people's salvation or their bane?

Prophesy is against them. Numbers, too. But, the greatest threat is mistrust. Can they forge an effective alliance before the bright power rising in the east destroys them?

The Unconquered Sun

Sequel to *A Bright Power Rising*.

Ever wish you were someone else? AscendantSun is about to…

He is beset by foes. The Harbinger's legions threaten the people he strives to defend. Critics among his own followers undermine him. The ambitions of his unreliable ally, Garscap Torp, endanger him at every turn. Worse, the blood-thirsty god he spurned is about to return. However, the greatest enemy he must face is himself.

The riddle set for him on the Crooked Stair will be answered on the bloody fields of Cliffringden. But will he survive it?

Acknowledgments

I want to thank Claire Ashgrove at Finish The Story for her editing skills. I also want to thank Pamela Guerrieri-Cangioli from Proofed To Perfection for proofreading it.

Thanks also must go to Paula Becattini who designed the beautiful cover of this book. I also want to thank those who took part in the poll to choose the cover—Colette Coughlan, Orla McGrath, Colm Murphy, Kate McAuliffe, Ian McInerney, D.E. Jackson, and the others who chose to remain anonymous.

I am also indebted as ever to Marina and Jason Anderson of Polgarus Studios for the formatting of the paperback.

About Noel Coughlan

I live with my wife and daughter in Ireland.

From a young age, I was always writing a book. Generally, the first page over and over. Sometimes, I even reached the second page before I had shredded the entire copy book.

In my teenage years, I wrote some poetry, some of which would make a Vogon blush.

When I was fourteen, I had a dream. It was of a world where the inhabitants believed that each hue of light was a separate god, and that matter was simply another form of light. Thus, the world of Elysion was born.

I tinkered with the idea for a couple of decades, putting together mythologies, histories, maps, etc., but world-building isn't worth much without a gripping story. Finally, I discovered a tale so compelling I just had to write it. The story was originally to be one book called *The Golden Rule*, but it expanded so much in the telling that I had to split it into two volumes, *A Bright Power Rising* and *The Unconquered Sun*.